Didi and Daddy on the Promenade

by Marilyn Singer
illustrated by Marie-Louise Gay

Clarion Books ⊚ New York

To my wonderful editor, Michele Coppola,
and her delightful son, Daniel.
—M.S.

The author would like to thank Steve Aronson,
Nadine Chang of the Brooklyn Heights Association,
Asher Williams, and the staff of Clarion Books.

Clarion Books
a Houghton Mifflin Company imprint
215 Park Avenue South, New York, NY 10003

Illustrations were executed in watercolor and pen and ink.
The text was set in 20-point Cochin.

www.houghtonmifflinbooks.com

Printed in Hong Kong

Library of Congress Cataloging-in-Publication Data
ISBN: 0-618-04640-2
LC#: 00-058977
Full cataloging information is available from the Library of Congress.

SCP 10 9 8 7 6 5 4 3 2 1

A NOTE FROM THE AUTHOR

Built in 1948–50 over a highway at the edge of Brooklyn, New York, the Brooklyn Heights Promenade is a walkway, almost a third of a mile long, that is bordered on one side by lovely houses and on the other by the East River. The Promenade—also known as the Esplanade—overlooks the Statue of Liberty, New York Harbor, lower Manhattan, and the Brooklyn Bridge. It offers a world-famous view of the magnificent Manhattan skyline.

Sunday morning, Didi jumps on Daddy's bed.
"Wake!" she says.
"Sleep." He yawns.
"Out!" she shouts.
"Pants!" he cries, tugging on his clothes.

5

She dashes outside.
"Didi, go slow!"
But Didi says, **"No!"**
She's in a hurry to get to the best place on earth.
She's in a hurry to get to the Promenade.

What will she see today?
A blue car? A yellow car?
A ship with a flag?

8

"Truck!" Didi yells. "Big white truck!"
"Boat," says Daddy. "Fat red boat."

10

Vroom!

12

"Vroom! Zoom!" roars Didi.
"Wide glide," says Daddy.
Side by side they pretend to ride. Then Didi speeds ahead.
"Didi, go slow!"
But Didi says, **"No!"**
Down the path she rumbles. Down the lively Promenade.

Zoom!

What will she greet today?
A pigeon? A squirrel?
A kitten on a fence?
"Puppy!" says Didi.
"Little yellow puppy."
"Dog!" says Daddy.
"Big black dog."

"Bow wow!" yips Didi.
"Woof boof!" Daddy answers.
They bark together.
Then Didi leaps ahead.
"Didi, go slow!"
But Didi says, **"No!"**
Away she races.
Down the busy Promenade.

17

What will she hear today?
A helicopter? A sea gull?
A radio tune?
"Drum!" says Didi. "Loud tall drum."
"Horn!" says Daddy. "Classy brassy horn."

Dance! Jump!

"Dance! Jump!" Didi twirls.
"Bebop hop!" Daddy spins.
Together they swing and swirl.
Daddy is fast, but Didi is faster.
"Didi, go slow!"
But Didi says, **"No!"**
Away she spins.
Down the noisy Promenade.

Who will she meet today?
Mr. Carson with his camera?
Officer Ann with her bike?
A baby with a ball?
"Chloe!" shouts Didi.
"Charlie!" Daddy says.

23

Swish! Slide!

24

Whish! Swing!

"Playground!" Didi squeals.
"Swish! Slide!"
"Playground!" hollers Chloe.
"Whish! Swing!"

"Sandbox," says Daddy. "Big dig."
They all climb into the sandbox.
"Beach!" says Didi. "Crowded beach."
"Beach!" says Daddy. "Cloudy beach.
It's starting to rain. Didi, let's go!"
But Didi says, **"No!"**
Out the gate she gallops.
To the end of the dizzy Promenade.

27

There's the highway and the river.
There's the sidewalk and the sky.
"Wet!" Didi laughs. "Giggly, wiggly wet!"
"Wet!" agrees Daddy. "Silly, chilly wet!"

29

Then boom, crash comes the thunder!
Zoom, flash comes the lightning!
It glows on the Statue of Liberty's crown.
Daddy grabs Didi's hand and starts to run home.
"Daddy, go slow!"
But Daddy says, **"No!"**
"Oh!" says Didi.

She laughs. Daddy laughs, too.

Away they fly, laughing and
splashing up the best place on earth.
Up the skippy, drippy, sparkly, parkly, perfect Promenade.